for Bill and Phyllis

Originally published as a jacketed hardcover by Philomel Books, a division of Penguin Young Readers Group, in 1984.
This edition published by World of Eric Carle, an imprint of Penguin Random House LLC, in 2020.

ERIC CARLE's name and signature logotype and the World of Eric Carle logo are trademarks of Eric Carle LLC.
Read Together, Be Together and the colophon are trademarks of Penguin Random House LLC.

Visit us online at penguinrandomhouse.com.
To find out more about Eric Carle and his books, please visit eric-carle.com.
To learn about The Eric Carle Museum of Picture Book Art, please visit carlemuseum.org.

The Library of Congress has cataloged the hardcover edition under the following Control Number: 84005907.
ISBN 978-0-399-21166-9 (hardcover) — ISBN 978-0-593-22424-3 (Read Together, Be Together)

Printed in the USA.
10 9 8 7 6 5 4 3 2 1

2020 Read Together, Be Together Edition

Eric Carle

The Very Busy Spider

world of
ERIC
CARLE

Early one morning the wind blew a spider across the field.
A thin, silky thread trailed from her body.
The spider landed on a fence post near a farm yard . . .

and began to spin a web with her silky thread.

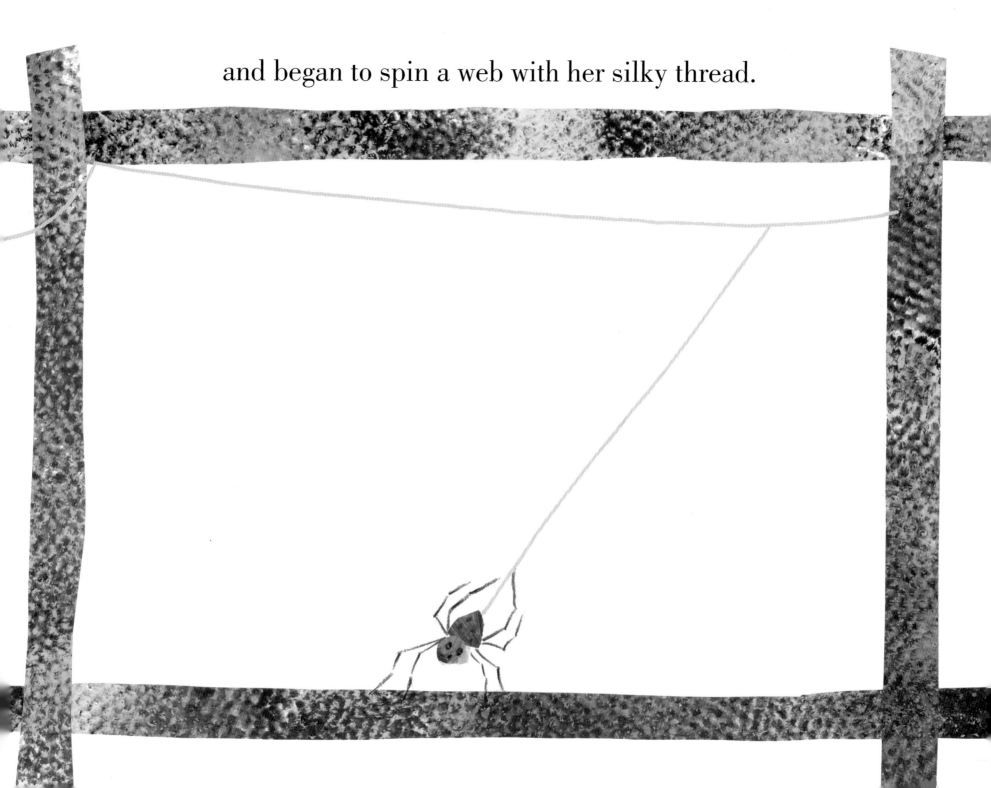

"Neigh! Neigh!" said the horse. "Want to go for a ride?"

The spider didn't answer. She was very busy spinning her web.

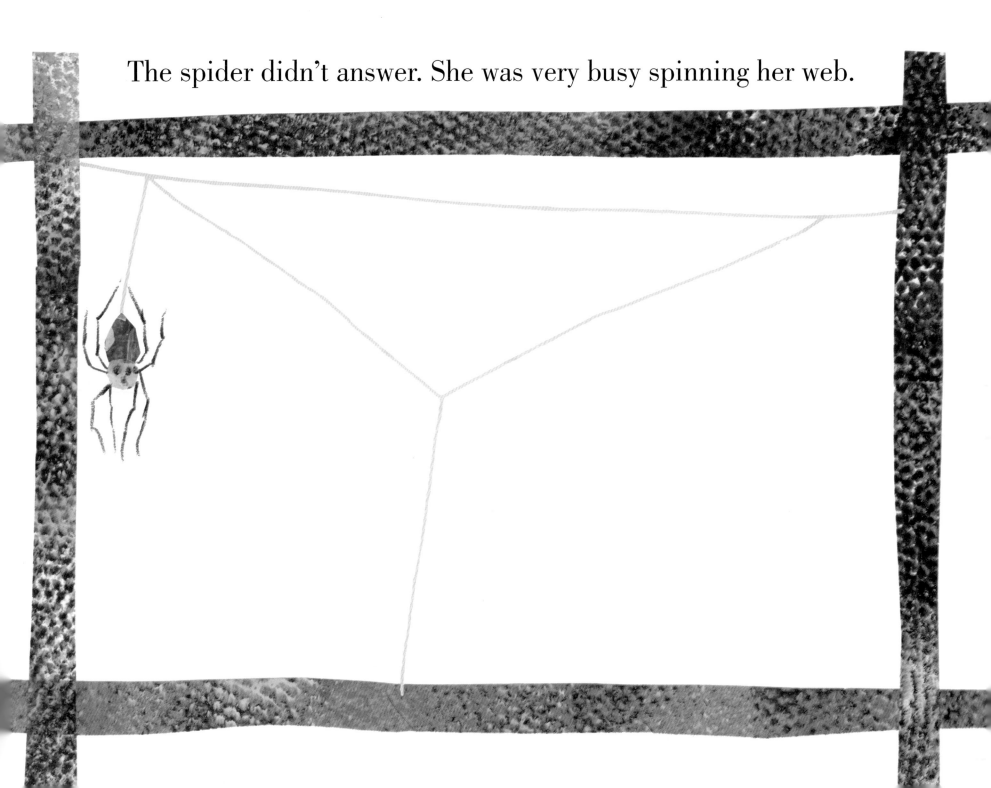

"Moo! Moo!" said the cow. "Want to eat some grass?"

The spider didn't answer. She was very busy spinning her web.

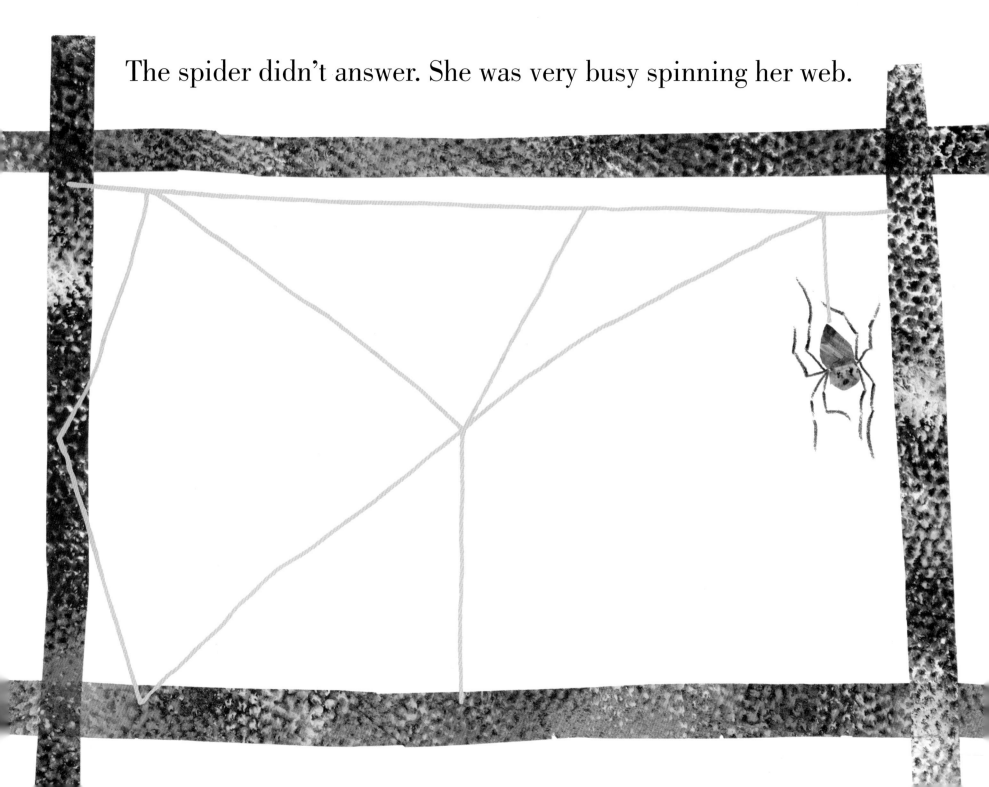

"Baa! Baa!" bleated the sheep. "Want to run in the meadow?"

The spider didn't answer. She was very busy spinning her web.

"Maa! Maa!" said the goat. "Want to jump on the rocks?"

The spider didn't answer. She was very busy spinning her web.

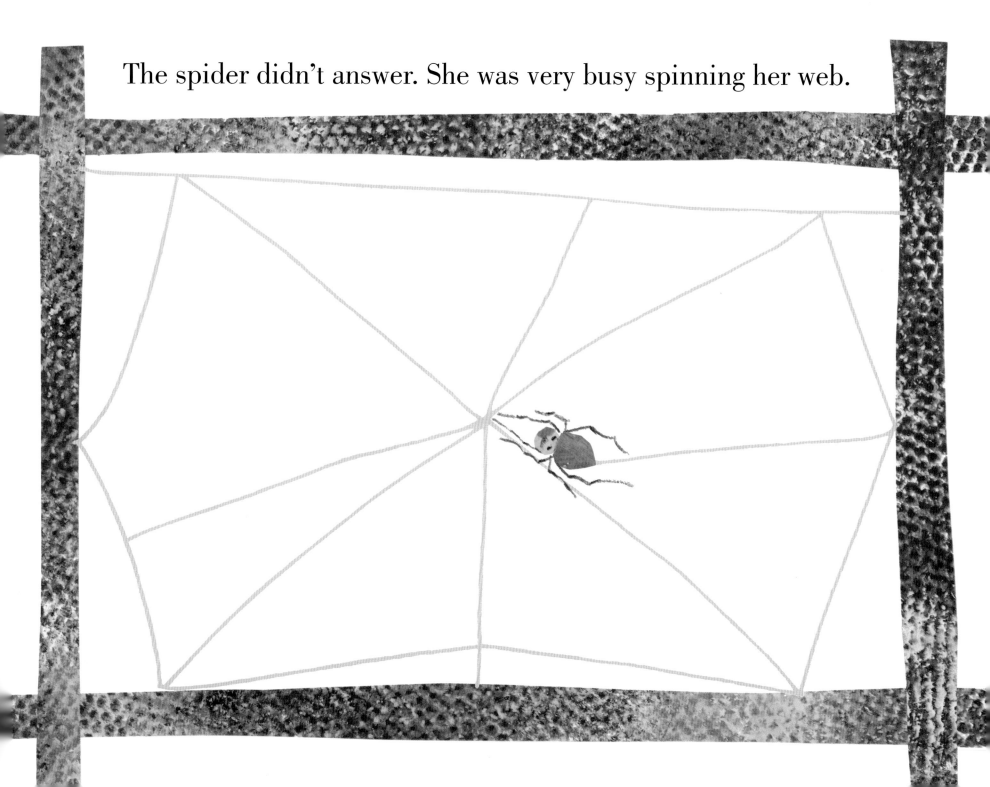

"Oink! Oink!" grunted the pig. "Want to roll in the mud?"

The spider didn't answer. She was very busy spinning her web.

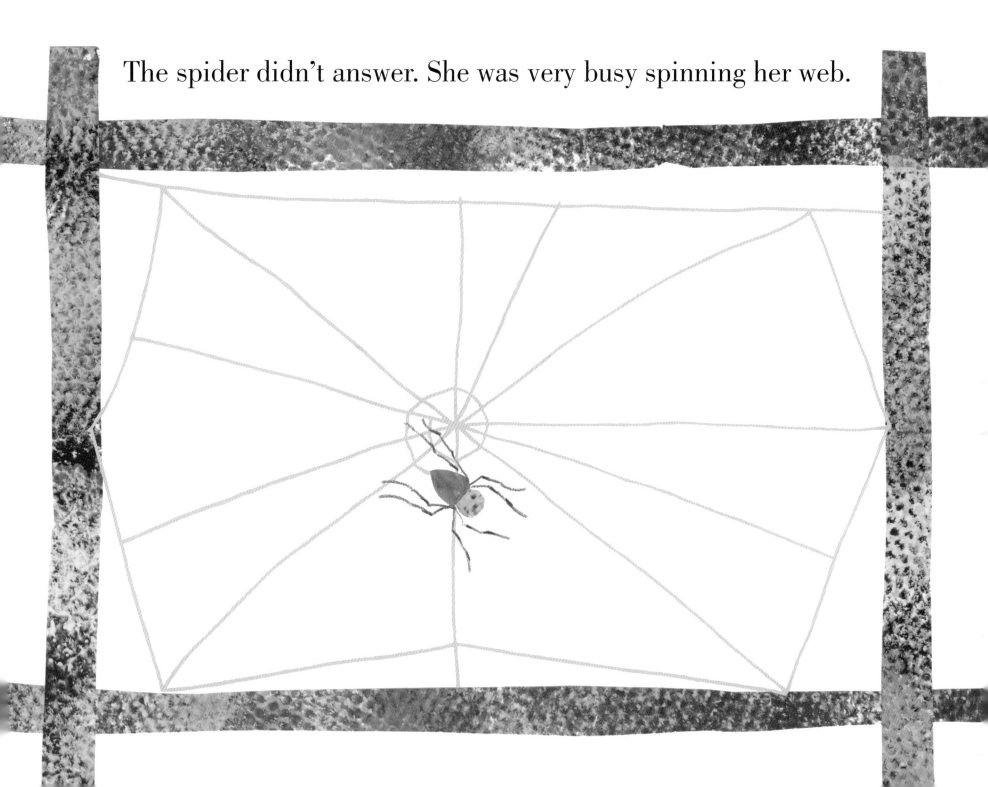

"Woof! Woof!" barked the dog. "Want to chase a cat?"

The spider didn't answer. She was very busy spinning her web.

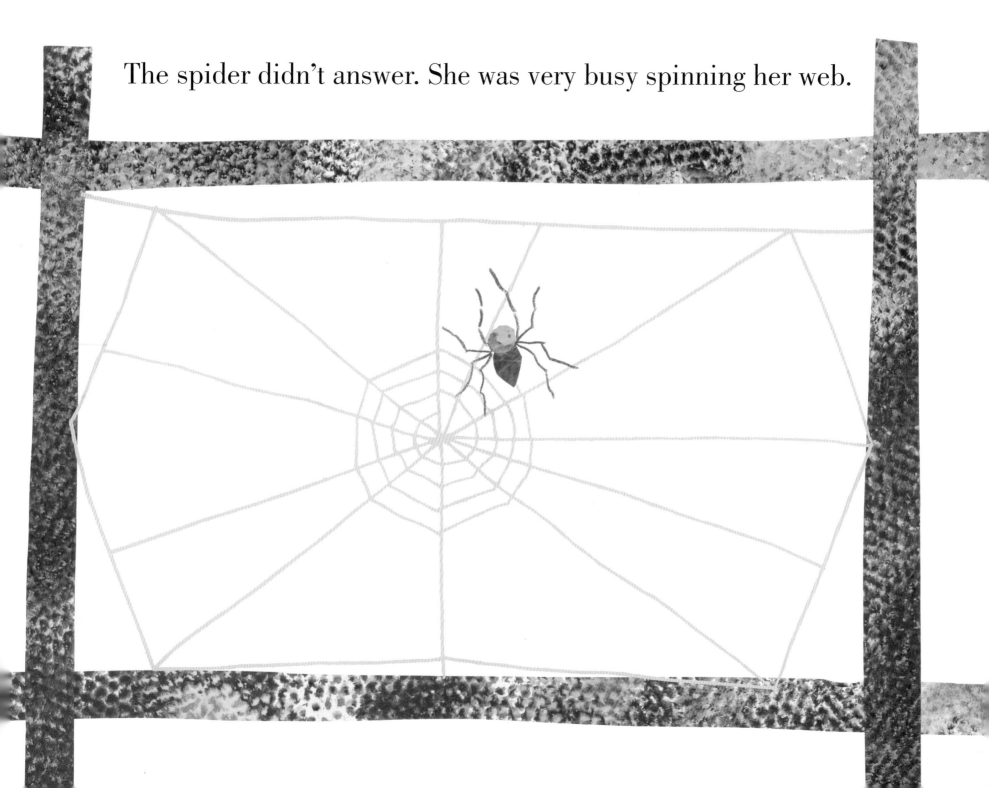

"Meow! Meow!" cried the cat. "Want to take a nap?"

The spider didn't answer. She was very busy spinning her web.

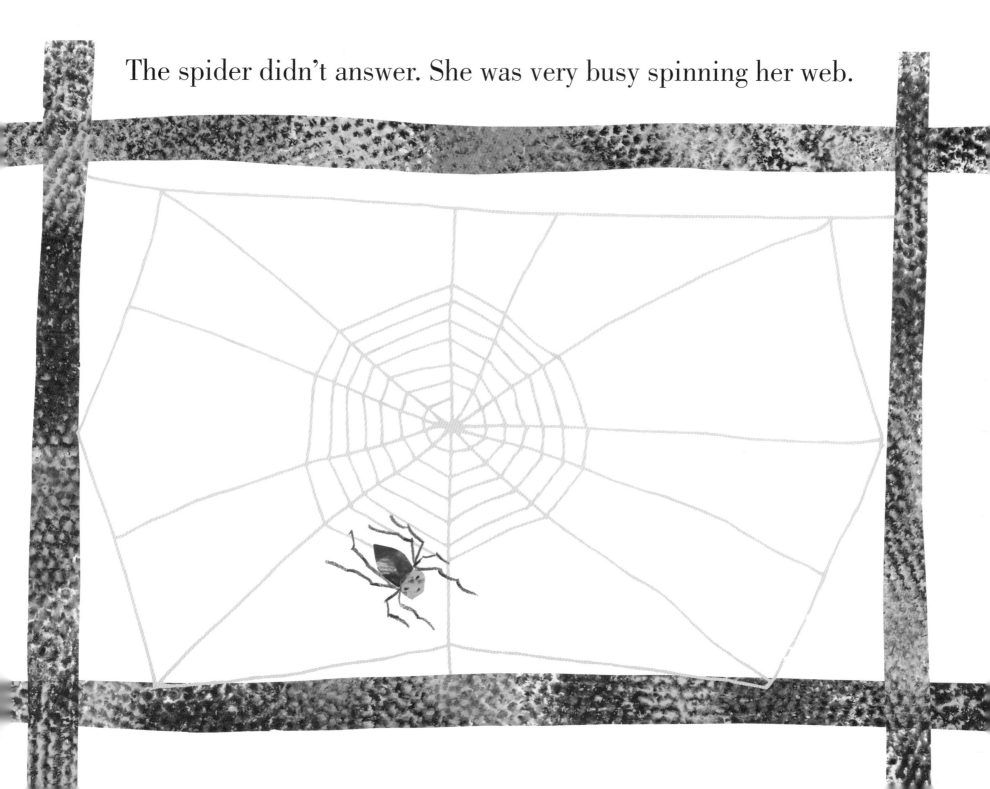

"Quack! Quack!" called the duck. "Want to go for a swim?"

The spider didn't answer. She had now finished her web.

"Cock-a-doodle do!" crowed the rooster. "Want to catch a pesty fly?"

And the spider caught the fly in her web . . . just like that!

"Whoo? Whoo?"
asked the owl.
"Who built this
beautiful web?"
The spider
didn't answer.
She had
fallen asleep.

It had been
a very, very
busy day.

8 Ways to Make the Most of Storytime

FROM THE EDITORS OF Parents.

① BE AS DRAMATIC AS POSSIBLE.

It'll help the story stick in your child's memory. You could give the mouse a British accent, make the lion roar, or speak very slowly when you're reading the snail's dialogue. Have fun making sound effects for words like boom, moo, or achoo. Encourage your child to act out movements, slithering like a snake or leaping like a frog.

② INVITE SPECIAL GUESTS.

Ask your kids if their favorite stuffed animal, action figure, or doll would like to listen too. Or curl up with the family pet. Including the whole gang will help hold their interest and make storytime seem more special. But if your child does start to lose interest before you've reached the last page, that's okay because half a book here or a quarter of a book there still counts as reading!

③ KEEP LOVINGLY WORN BOOKS IN THE ROTATION.

There's a reason your kids ask for the same title again and again: A familiar story can be as comforting as a favorite blankie. The characters become their friends, and the books serve an important emotional purpose.

④ PLAY A GUESSING GAME.

When reading a new book, pause a few times to challenge your kids to predict what's going to happen next. Encourage them to refer to the title and illustrations for clues.

⑤ REFLECT ON THE STORY.

Talk about a book for a few minutes before you move on to another. Start a conversation with statements like "I'm wondering…," "I wish I could ask the author…," and "I'm getting the idea…" This helps develop your children's intuition and their ability to communicate a story back to you.

⑥ CONNECT STORIES WITH WHAT'S HAPPENING IN REAL LIFE.

Suppose you read your child a story about a baby bird, and a day or two later, you spot a tiny sparrow in the park. Ask your child, "Doesn't that bird look like the one in the book we read yesterday? I wonder if it's looking for its mommy too?" Doing so will help promote information recall and build vocabulary.

⑦ CREATE AN IMPROVISED READING NOOK.

Storytime on the sofa or a cozy chair is sweet, but wouldn't your kids lose their mind if you set up a fort every now and then? It doesn't have to be fancy: Just drape a blanket over two chairs, grab a couple of pillows, and squeeze in.

⑧ ALWAYS BE THE STORYTELLER AT BEDTIME.

You'll feel so proud when your little ones start recognizing and sounding out words on their own. But resist asking them to read to you at bedtime because it would replace this warm, wonderful bonding ritual with something that can feel like work for kids. Plus, they'll be able to listen to a more complicated book than they can read on their own.

READ TOGETHER, BE TOGETHER is a nationwide movement developed by Penguin Random House in partnership with *Parents* magazine that celebrates the importance, and power, of the shared reading experience between an adult and a child. Reading aloud regularly to babies and young children is one of the most effective ways to foster early literacy and is a key factor responsible for building language and social skills. READ TOGETHER, BE TOGETHER offers parents the tips and tools to make family reading a regular and cherished activity.